What any author wants is for his books to become dog-eared and familiar. I've been lucky enough that my very young readers are particularly adept at giving their books doggy ears in no time at all.

And of all my books, perhaps it's those about Kipper that get the doggiest ears of all, which I guess is kind of appropriate.

Mick Inkpen

More books about Kipper

Kipper's Toybox
Kipper's Birthday
Kipper's Snowy Day
Kipper's Christmas Eve
Kipper's A to Z
Kipper and Roly
Kipper's Monster
Kipper's Beach Ball
One Year with Kipper
Hide Me, Kipper
Kipper Story Collection
Kipper's Birthday and
Other Stories

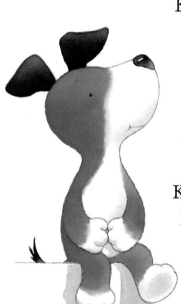

First published in 1991
by Hodder Children's Books

This edition published in 2014

Text and illustrations copyright © Mick Inkpen 1991

Hodder Children's Books
338 Euston Road
London NW1 3BH

Hodder Children's Books Australia
Level 17/207 Kent Street
Sydney, NSW 2000

A catalogue record of this book is available
from the British Library.

ISBN: 978 1 444 91816 8
10 9 8 7 6 5 4 3

Printed in China

Hodder Children's Books is a division of
Hachette Children's Books.
An Hachette UK Company.
www.hachette.co.uk

Kipper

Mick Inkpen

Hodder
Children's
Books

A division of Hachette Children's Books

Kipper was in the mood for tidying his basket.

'You are falling apart!' he said to his rabbit.

'You are chewed and you are soggy!' he said to his ball and his bone.

'And you are DISGUSTING!' he said to his smelly old blanket.

Out they went.
'That's better!' said Kipper.

But it was not better. Now his
basket was uncomfortable.
He twisted and he turned.
He wiggled and he wriggled.
But it was no good. He could
not get comfortable.
    'Silly basket!' said Kipper…

…and went outside.

Outside there were two ducks.
They looked very comfortable
standing on one leg.

'That's what I should do!' said
Kipper. But he wasn't very good.
He could only...

...wobble.

Some wrens had made a nest inside a flowerpot. It looked very cosy.

'I should sleep in one of those!' said Kipper. But Kipper would not fit inside a flowerpot.

He was much too big!

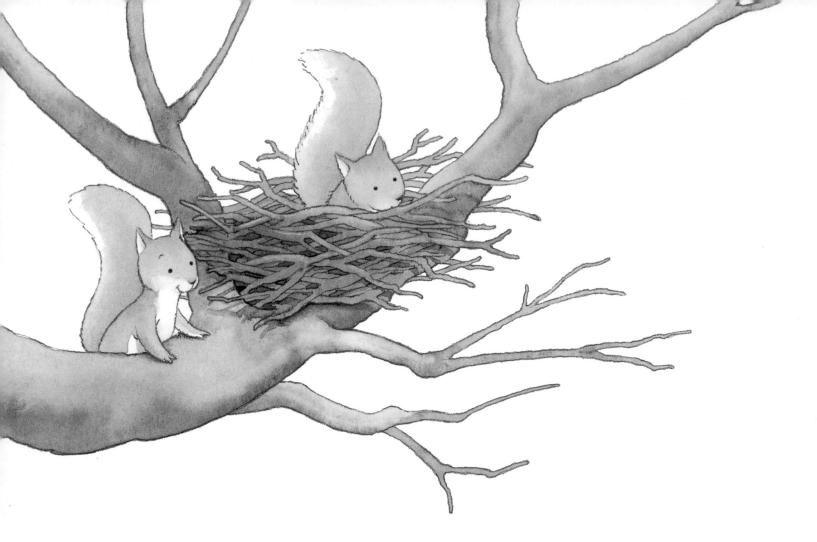

The squirrels had made their nest
out of sticks.
  'I will build myself a stick nest!'
said Kipper. But Kipper's nest was
not very good. He could only find…

...three sticks!

The sheep looked very happy
just sitting in the grass.
No, that was no good either.
The grass was much too…

...tickly!

The frog had found a sunny
place in the middle of the pond.
He was sitting on a lily pad.
   'I wonder if I could do that,'
said Kipper.

But he couldn't!

'Perhaps a nice dark hole would be good,' thought Kipper. 'The rabbits seem to like them.'

But it was not
a rabbit hole!

Kipper rushed indoors and hid underneath his blanket.

His

lovely

old

smelly

blanket!

Kipper put the blanket back in his basket. He found his rabbit.

'Sorry Rabbit,' he said.
He found his bone and his ball.

'I like my basket just the way it is,' yawned Kipper. He climbed in and pulled the blanket over his head.

'It's the best basket in the whole, wide…'

. . .sssssssssssssshh

hhhhhhh!

'My children absolutely LOVE all of Mick Inkpen's books, and I still love reading Kipper to them, even when it's for the hundredth time. . .'

CRESSIDA COWELL

'He is the perfect pup to grow up with. . .'

HILARY MCKAY

'Storytelling at its best.' DAVID MELLING